DANNY DOLLAR
MILLIONAIRE EXTRAORDINAIRE

BY TY JACKSON

THE LEMONADE ESCAPADE

Published by Big Head Books

Library of Congress Control Number: 2010914670

ISBN: 978-0-615-39517-3

Printed in the U.S.A.

WOR 20 10

To you,
Yeah, you!

DREAM BIGGER!

There is nothing **YOU** can't do!
Now get bookin'!!!

DANNY DOLLAR MILLIONAIRE EXTRAORDINAIRE©

The Lemonade Escapade
By Ty Allan Jackson

Let Me Introduce Myself

Danny Dollar, Millionaire. Yes, you read it right, MILLIONAIRE!!! Ok, I'm not a millionaire yet, but I'm gonna be!

Yep, this little knucklehead kid is gonna make it big. Not only will I become a millionaire, I've got a plan to do it by the time I'm 21 years old. That's about 10 years from now. And I'll tell you how I'm gonna do it in one word: INVESTING! That's right, I said investing. Okay, you might be asking yourself, "What the heck is investing?" Well, I'll tell you. But first, a little bit about me.

I live in the Eastchester section of the Bronx, New York along with my Mom, Dad, and older sister.

I'm your typical kid; I love music, I really love basketball, but the thing I love the most is, well, money. Now I know everyone loves money, but not like me. I'm a money maniac. I love money like other kids love candy. I know everything there is to know about money. For example, did you know that the first forms of money were animals, like cows? Yep, cows! People would trade cattle and other animals for things that they wanted. That's called *bartering*.

Bartering is when you trade something you have for something you want. Imagine going to the sneaker store and telling the guy behind the counter:

"Yo, I'll give you three cows for these sneakers."

"With tax it comes up to three cows and two chickens."

Dang! That would be crazy!

In case you're wondering how I earn the money that I love so much, well DUH, I have a job! Actually, I've got a few jobs. I walk Mrs. Gonzalez's dogs before and after school. *Cha-Ching!* I go to the store for Mr. Milton every other day; he's kinda old. *Cha-Ching!* I rake leaves in the fall, shovel snow in the winter, wash cars and mow lawns in the summer, *Cha-Ching,*

Cha-Ching, Cha-Ching! You get the picture. By the end of the week, I'm hauling in about one hundred dollars. That's serious paper for an 11-year-old kid.

Every Saturday I'm off to my favorite place in the world, THE BANK! Yep, the bank. The people there are crazy cool. As soon as I walk in, the security guard, Mr. Block, always says, "Dollar Dan, the Man with the plan." And I say, "Mr. Block, got the bank on lock." I really like that dude.

Then, I go to the same teller, Mrs. Susan Anthony. She always greets me with "Good morning, Mr. Dollar." Mr. Dollar! Man, do I like the sound of that! I deposit all I've earned throughout the week, except for ten dollars that I keep for playing around with. After Mrs. Anthony updates my bankbook, I give her a little wink, she winks back, and it's a wrap. I'm done. I'm almost floating on the way back home thinking about how much money I've saved. And what I'm saving for is awesome. It's big, it's huge, it's colossal! It's part of my goal to becoming a millionaire. Okay, okay, okay…I'll tell you.

You know how some kids want to be a big-time basketball player? Well not me, I want to be a big-time basketball team owner, just like my idol Rocky Austin. Mr. Austin started out flippin' burgers as a kid and now owns a billion dollar fast food chain called "Flippin' Burgers" and he owns the Texas Mustangs basketball team, too. So, now you've got it. I want to own a basketball team. That's my dream! How am I gonna get enough money to own a basketball team? I told you earlier—INVESTING!

Here's the plan, so pay attention: investing means taking your money and buying something that will make you more money, like a stock or a bond. With stock, you pay money to a company and then you actually own a small part of that company, for example, the Yola-Cola Company. They make my favorite soft drink. Let's say I own stock in Yola-Cola. When they make a lot of money I get a piece, so the more stock that I own, the bigger the piece

I get. If Yola-Cola doesn't make money, I could lose some of the money I've invested. Sounds risky I know, but like my Dad always says, "No risk, no reward."

A bond is a little less risky than buying stock. With a bond, you let a business or the government borrow your money and they promise to give that money back with interest. Interest is money they give you for letting them borrow your money. Sometimes, I loan my big-head sister five bucks and I charge her two bucks to borrow my five bucks. When she pays me back, she has to give me seven bucks. I just made two bucks in interest for loaning her only five. Get it?! Sounds cool, right? (Although sometimes she tries to jerk me out of my two bucks, so I hold her diary hostage. HAHA, it works every time).

So, I take most of the money that I earn and put it into the bank or invest it into stocks and bonds. The money I earn in interest or by investing, I reinvest into other things. That's called diversifying. Diversifying is when you invest your money into different things to try and make more money. ARE YOU GETTING ALL OF THIS?!

I know it's a lot to swallow; you should have seen me trying to explain all this to my parents. Their heads are still spinning. But when they're sitting in the skybox watching my team win a championship, I'm sure they'll say to each other, "That

Yola-Cola stock really paid off!"

Yep, one day I'm gonna be a millionaire. I'll be a successful Wall Street investor who owns a professional basketball team; who gives to charities and helps those less fortunate; who conquers the global financial industry. I'm gonna achieve all my goals and dreams. But being a future millionaire isn't easy. There's a lot of responsibility that goes with being "Dan, the Man." Responsibility and sacrifice. But until I become a millionaire, I've got poop to pick up.

Let me explain. Just the other day, I was playing basketball with the guys when the alarm on my watch went off. It was four o'clock and time for me to walk Mrs.

Gonzalez's dogs. We were winning thirty to twenty; the game was intense. The guys begged me not to go, but I made a promise to Mrs. Gonzalez that I would be on time. It was her bingo night and she couldn't be late, so I couldn't be late. That meant leaving before the game was over. I had my friend Noogie take my place playing ball, which did not make the guys on my team happy. They called me a peanut head. Can you believe that?! But I would rather be called a peanut head than be called irresponsible. Because of Noogie, my team lost the game thirty to forty. After I left, they didn't score another point, and they called ME a peanut head?!

When I got to Mrs. G's house, those

dogs were buggin' out! There are three of them, all Chihuahuas: Nina, Pinta, and Santa Maria.

Walking them was a nightmare. First, Nina picked a fight with a huge pit bull. She was barking like that dog owed her money. The funny thing was that the pit bull backed down. You had to see it to believe it. Then, Pinta had an accident on Pablo's new sneakers.

Pablo is the neighborhood bully. He was furious and vowed he would get me back. I told him that it wasn't my fault; a dog's gotta do what a dog's gotta do. As I walked away, I shouted, "Pee you later." HAHA! He didn't like that at all.

To make things worse, Santa Maria

got loose and decided to chase pigeons. Then, the pigeons decided to use her as target practice. Guess who had to give Santa Maria a bath? Yep, peanut head! Did I mention having to pick up their poop? Oh well, it was worth it. Mrs. G. gave me ten bucks for walking her dogs plus a five dollar tip for washing Santa Maria. *Cha-ching!* That's fifteen dollars for about one hour of work. Not bad, but that's nothing compared to the money I'll make with the lemonade stand that I've got planned.

Chapter 1
Pablo's Woes

"Yo Noogie, pass me the ball," Danny yelled.

"Try and get it!" teased Noogie.

"Alright, that's enough playing around. Let's get a real game going. Come on, two on two. Me and Benjamin against Andrew and Noogie," Danny screamed out.

"Why do I always get stuck with Noogie?" asked Andrew.

"Cause you both stink!" said Benjamin, as he made a perfect jump shot.

The ball sank into the hoop then rolled across the court, where it was picked up by Pablo. Pablo stepped onto the court followed by his boys, Washington and

Fingers. He ignored the other boys and passed the ball to Washington, who then passed it to Fingers.

"Hey, give us the ball back," yelled Benjamin.

"If you want it, come and get it chumps!" Pablo yelled back. Noogie tried to grab the ball and accidentally stepped on Pablo's new sneakers.

"YO, ARE YOU CRAZY?! I just paid a hundred dollars for these kicks!" Pablo screamed.

"You paid one hundred bucks for a pair of sneakers, you got played!" said Danny.

"You're just mad because my sneakers are nicer than yours, and I didn't

get played, my Moms bought them for
me!" said Pablo. Danny thought to himself,
*'Mom said Pablo's mother just get laid off
from work. How could she spend one
hundred dollars on a pair of sneakers?'*

"Let's get outta here and let the girls play their little basketball game," Pablo said, as he threw the ball hard at Andrew.

"Man, that dude has a serious attitude problem," said Andrew.

"Yeah, he's got issues," Danny responded.

Later at Pablo's house, Pablo yelled, "Yo, Mom, what's for dinner? I'm starving."

"Grilled cheese," his mom replied with a sigh.

"Are you kidding me, grilled cheese again? We've had grilled cheese three times this week. Can I at least have two?"

"No honey, grilled cheese is all we can

afford, and we only have enough for two, one for you and one for me." Pablo thought to himself as he looked down at the scuff on his new sneakers, '*Man, all my Mom can afford for us to eat are grilled cheese sandwiches. Maybe I shouldn't have begged her to buy me these sneakers.*'

DANNY'S DID YOU KNOW?

DID YOU KNOW THAT WE CALL MONEY "BUCKS" BECAUSE BEFORE THERE WAS PAPER MONEY, AMERICANS USED TO BARTER ANIMALS LIKE DEER AND ELKS? GET IT? BUCKS

Chapter 2
Twisted Sister

"How much did you deposit today, Son?" asked Dad Dollar.

"Eighty-seven dollars, *Cha-Ching!*" Danny yelled.

"How does this wannabe tycoon make all this money?" Danielle asked.

"Your brother works very hard for his money with his odd jobs. You should get an afterschool job yourself and not rely on just your allowance," Mom Dollar said.

"By the way, Mom can I have an advance on my allowance? Tonya and Denise want to go to the movies tonight. All I need is twenty bucks."

"I just gave you an advance last week, and you're not getting another," Dad Dollar said sternly. Danielle turned to Danny.

"Hey Danny, you think you could loan me twenty dollars 'til next week?"

"Sure, at twenty percent *interest**," Danny said with a smug look on his face.

"Twenty percent, last time it was ten

percent! Why's it twenty now?"

"Twenty percent is the weekend rate. Take it or leave it."

"I can't believe this is happening!" Danielle screamed, as Mom and Dad busted out laughing.

Later that evening, Dad Dollar walked into the living room to find Danny watching TV.

"Hey, what are you watching?"

"I'm flipping back and forth between, "Young Rich Entrepreneurs" on the Finance Network and the New York Ballers basketball game," Danny said.

"You are, huh? Danny, I've been meaning to talk to you about all this finance mumbo-jumbo and working so much."

"Dad, my jobs don't interfere with my school work! You know I'm one of the best students in school! I love working and saving, plus learning all this financial stuff is preparing me for my future. I'm going to be a millionaire, Dad! I wanna own a basketball team so bad I can…"

"Wait, hold on Danny. I only wanted to tell you how proud I am of you. You're an incredible kid, I mean young man. I wish I had your work ethic and business savvy when I was your age; maybe then we wouldn't be so…never mind. I just want to say, keep up the good work, Son. One other thing, one of my co-workers suggested that I should take the money in our savings account and put it into a *CD***. That's not the disc that plays music, is it?"

"No Dad, it's not that kind of CD. First, let's get some cookies and milk and then I'll break it down for you."

*Remember, interest is the price paid for using someone else's money.

**A CD, which stands for Certificate of Deposit, is a special type of savings account. With a CD, you cannot take out your money whenever you want. It must stay in the account for a certain amount of time or you pay a penalty. But, the interest you gain is much greater than in a regular savings account.

More interest = more money for you. CHA-CHING!

DANNY'S DID YOU KNOW?

DID YOU KNOW THAT THE LARGEST BILL EVER PRINTED WAS A $100,000 BILL? IT WAS ONLY USED IN THE 1930'S, AND WOODROW WILSON WAS THE PRESIDENT DEPICTED ON THE BILL. CAN YOU IMAGINE GOING TO THE GROCERY STORE AND ASKING THE CASHIER IF THEY HAVE CHANGE FOR ONE HUNDRED THOUSAND DOLLARS WHEN YOU ONLY WANT TO BUY A PACK OF GUM? IF THE CASHIER DIDN'T HAVE CHANGE, YOU COULD TELL THEM, "MAYBE I'LL JUST BUY THE STORE!"

Chapter 3
Cha-Church

It's nine o'clock on Sunday morning; Danny yawned, jumped out of bed and headed to the bathroom.

"Another day, another dollar!" he said, winking at himself in the bathroom mirror.

"Mom! What time is church?" Danny asked.

"Same time every Sunday, ten o'clock, so shake your tail feather. We're all ready to go, sleepy head."

By ten-fifteen, the Dollars were seated at the Heavenly Spirit Church. While Pastor Johnson was dramatically delivering his sermon, Danny scribbled in his notebook.

"What are you doing?" Dad Dollar whispered.

"I'm going over my list of jobs to do after church. I'm walking Mrs. Gonzalez's dogs at one o'clock, helping clean the community center at two, and then mowing grass 'til three-thirty."

"Do you have to do that now?" Dad whispered sternly.

"How can I be Dan, the Man, if I don't have a plan? *Cha-Ching!*"

"Something is wrong with this boy," sighed Dad Dollar.

"That's your son," Mom Dollar said.

Danny is completely distracted by his list until Pastor Johnson announces that they are taking an offering for charity to feed the homeless people in the community.

"Oooh great, I love giving to charities," Danny said.

"Why is that?" Mom Dollar asked.

"It gives me a warm feeling inside knowing that I'm helping those who are less fortunate. I know if I needed help, I would want someone to help me. When I give to charities I feel like I'm doing my part to help other people, not to mention, it's a tax write-off."

"Now that's my son," Dad Dollar said proudly.

DANNY'S DID YOU KNOW

DID YOU KNOW THAT BILL GATES, FOUNDER OF MICROSOFT, AND HIS WIFE MELINDA HAVE GIVEN OVER 28 BILLION DOLLARS TO CHARITY? WOW! I'M SURE THE "THANK YOU" CARD THEY RECEIVED WAS REALLY NICE!

Chapter 4
Shoes or Lose

It's five o'clock and dinnertime at the Dollars. Mom, Dad, Danielle and Danny are sitting down for Sunday dinner.

"So Danielle, where did you and Tonya go after church today?" asked Mom Dollar.

"We just went to the mall. There was a big sale on shoes that I could not pass up."

"Shoes?!" Danny, Mom and Dad all shouted at the same time.

"Child, you can't possibly fit another pair of shoes in that closet of yours," Mom Dollar said. "Where did you get the money to buy a pair of shoes anyway? You just borrowed money from your brother yesterday!"

"At twenty percent interest," Danny boasted with a smile.

"Hush, Danny," Mom Dollar said.

"I borrowed money from Tonya," Danielle said with her head down.

"Baby, you can't continue to borrow money, especially when you can't afford to pay it back."

"I'll pay back Tonya and Danny, I promise."

"Danielle, it will take you a month to pay them both back with your allowance and that's only if you don't spend money on anything else. That's how people get into *debt**. They continue to spend money through loans or *credit cards*** that they can't afford to pay back," said Mom

Dollar.

"So what?" Danielle asked.

"So what?! Often, when loans and credit cards aren't paid, the things you bought are taken away, and you still have to pay the bill. Even worse, your credit history is destroyed," said Dad Dollar.

"What's a credit history?" Danielle asked.

"It's like a report card, but instead of grading your school work it grades how you manage your money. Every one has one. If you have a good credit score, you can get loans from a bank so you can buy a house, car or get money for college at a really low interest rate. If your credit score is low, then you're charged a really high interest rate or you're denied loans altogether. A bad credit score makes lenders think you won't be able to pay back their money," Dad Dollar explained.

"Danielle, you want to buy a car someday, don't you?" Mom Dollar asked.

"You know I do."

"Well, how will you afford to buy a car if you're always in debt?"

"Mom, it's just Danny and Tonya."

"Yes, and you're paying twenty percent interest to Danny. Not smart money management, honey."

"Looks like you'll be taking the bus 'til you're forty," Danny snickered.

"This is the second time I'm telling you to hush, boy!"

"Sorry, Mom." Danny said respectfully.

"Let me ask you a question. Are you broke?"

"Yes," Danielle said shamefully.

"Do you like being broke?"

"No, of course not."

"Then what is your plan to get back on track?"

"My plan? I really don't have a plan, but since my allowance isn't enough to pay Danny and Tonya back right away, I better look into getting a job. I heard the library is hiring. I'll go there after school tomorrow. Then maybe the little tycoon-buffoon over there can take me to his bank and show me how to open a savings account."

"WHO ARE YOU CALLING A BUFFOON?!" yelled Danny.

"What about the shoes?" Dad Dollar asked.

"What about them? Those shoes are hot!"

"If you return the shoes, you could give Tonya back her money, and then you would just have to pay your brother." Reluctantly, Danielle agreed.

"If I take the shoes back, do I still have to look for a job?"

Danny giggled and rubbed his hands together greedily.

"You better get a job because the next time you need a loan, The Bank of Danny's interest rate is going up to thirty percent. That's called *inflatio*n,*** look it up!"

* *Debt is when you owe something, usually money, to another person or company.*

***A credit card is a plastic card issued by a bank or store that allows someone to buy things now and pay for them later. The problem is the credit card company charges you interest for borrowing their money, which can lead to debt.*

Debt = CHA-CHUMP

*** *Inflation is a rise in the cost of goods or services.*

DANNY'S DID YOU KNOW?

DID YOU KNOW THERE ARE MORE THAN SEVEN MILLION MILLIONAIRES IN THE WORLD TODAY? THAT MEANS THERE IS ABOUT ONE MILLIONAIRE FOR EVERY 1000 PEOPLE. MAN, THERE ARE MORE MILLIONAIRES AROUND THAN I THOUGHT.

Chapter 5
The Man with the Plan

Yawn! "Another day, another dollar!" Danny said as he walked into the kitchen.

"Good morning, honey. What are you going to have for breakfast? We have eggs, pancakes, bacon, fruit and grits. What's it going to be?"

"I'm just gonna have some fruit Mom; I've got to get moving. It's going to be a big day."

"Why, what have you got planned?" asked Dad Dollar.

"He's probably going to sell one of Mrs. Gonzalez's dogs for a buck," said Danielle.

"That's ninety-nine cents more than I would get for you," replied Danny.

"All right, all right, that's enough you two. What do you have planned today, Danny?" asked Mom Dollar.

"Today there's a big festival in the neighborhood. The guys and I are gonna sell lemonade, but not just any old lemonade. We're gonna sell the world's greatest lemonade. We're using shaved ice, umbrellas in the cups and making different flavors of lemonade, too. It'll be awesome."

"That's a great idea, honey. Maybe your sister could help you," Mom Dollar said.

"What?! I wouldn't help Lemonhead sell lemonade for all the money in the world," shouted Danielle.

"That's fine with me. I've got Benjamin

and Noogie helping me."

"Noogie! That kid is crazy, and what kind of name is Noogie anyway?" asked Danielle.

"His real name is Abraham. We call him Noogie because he has a small lump on his head. Besides, they're willing to work for free while you'll probably want a doggie treat, right Fido?"

"You two have got to cut it out," said Dad Dollar.

DANNY'S DID YOU KNOW?

DID YOU KNOW ONE OF THE YOUNGEST SELF-MADE MILLIONAIRES IS FARRAH GRAY, WHO WAS ON WELFARE AT AGE SIX? TO EARN MONEY, HE SOLD LOTIONS AND PAINTED ROCKS DOOR TO DOOR. THROUGH HARD WORK AND DETERMINATION, HE MADE HIS FIRST MILLION BY AGE 14. FARRAH IS CURRENTLY A COLUMNIST, AUTHOR, AND REAL ESTATE CEO. MAN, I BET HE COULD PLAY ONE MEAN GAME OF MONOPOLY.

Chapter 6
Stand by Me

"This lemonade stand is a great idea Danny. I wish I'd thought of it. There must be about twenty-five people in line. What made you think of selling lemonade?" asked Benjamin.

"I knew there would be a lot of people coming out for the festival, and who can resist a little kid selling lemonade? It's about ninety degrees out here, so everybody's hot and thirsty, plus I knew no one else would think of it. We've only been out here for an hour and already made a hundred bucks. *Cha-Ching!* This is going to be my biggest payday ever," said Danny.

Danny heard a commotion and noticed Pablo, Washington and Fingers cutting to the front of the line.

"Well, well, well, what have we got here? Looks like Danny's got a little Cool-Aid stand going on," said Pablo.

"It's a lemonade stand," said Danny.

"Lemonade, Cool-Aid, whatever! You're gonna need a band aid if you're not careful. Don't think I forgot about what that dog did to my sneakers," said Pablo.

"It was an accident. Here, have a cup of lemonade, on the house."

"No thanks, chump. You can keep your stinking lemonade. We're outta here! Come on guys."

"Man, you know what Pablo and your

lemonade have in common, Danny?" asked Noogie. "They're both sour."

As Pablo walked away, he whispered to Washington and Fingers, "I know how we can get that chump back for messing up my sneakers."

DANNY'S DID YOU KNOW?

DID YOU KNOW THE FIRST AMERICAN MILLIONAIRE WAS FUR TRADER JOHN JACOB ASTOR, BORN IN 1763? THE FIRST AMERICAN FEMALE MILLIONAIRE WAS AFRICAN-AMERICAN BUSINESSWOMAN AND HAIR CARE ENTREPRENEUR, MADAM C.J. WALKER, BORN IN 1867. YOU GO, GIRL!

Chapter 7
Pablo's Revenge

"Young man, you are some entrepreneur. This is the best lemonade I've ever had. What did you put in it?" asked a customer.

"Ma'am, it's very simple, I use freshly squeezed lemons, sugar, and my special ingredient, but it's a family secret, so I can't tell you," said Danny. "I'm glad you like it. Please come again, and tell your friends."

"Hey Danny, what did that lady call you?" asked Noogie.

"She called me an entrepreneur. That's a person who runs their own business."

"Oh, I thought she said it tastes like manure."

"Noogie, you're a nut," laughed Benjamin.

"Oh brother, there goes Pablo and Washington cutting the line again." said Noogie.

"You know what? I think we'll take that lemonade after all; it is kinda hot out here." said Pablo.

"Here you go Pablo, no hard feelings about your sneakers, right? Here's one for you and one for Washington and Fingers…hey, where is Fingers?"

"I don't know. He must be around here somewhere."

"Well, when you see him, tell him he's got a cup on the house."

"Yeah, OK, see you later," said Pablo.

"Maybe Pablo's not a bad guy after all," Danny wondered aloud.

Little did Danny know, Pablo was distracting them so Fingers could pour a bottle of vinegar into their last container of lemonade.

Chapter 8
Lemon-paid

"Wow, so far we've gone through five containers of lemonade and we have one more left," exclaimed Noogie.

"This has to be the most money I've ever made in one day. Benji, what's the total amount we've made so far?" asked Danny.

"We've sold 327 cups of lemonade at one dollar apiece. That's $327. Can you believe we made $327 in one day!? That is a big payday," said Benjamin excitedly.

"This is awesome guys. We made a *net profit** of $246." said Danny.

"What do you mean by net profit?" Noogie asked as he scratched his head.

"Have you ever heard the saying, 'It takes money to make money'?"

"Yeah, I've heard that before, never figured out what it meant though." said Noogie.

"It's true; I had to spend my own money to set up this lemonade stand. I had to buy the containers to put the lemonade in, the cups, the ice, the little umbrellas and the ingredients to make the lemonade. All those things are called *expenses*. Expenses are the monies spent to create and run a business. Once your business makes money, like the $327 we made today, you subtract your expenses. I spent $81 of my own money, remember that?" Noogie and Benjamin both nodded their heads.

"Subtract that from the total we made and it gives us a net profit of $246."

"Oh, I get it!" said Benjamin.

"Spend money to make money! Now it makes sense!" beamed Noogie.

"There's just one last expense, payroll. That means paying you guys for helping me out."

"We told you we would help you out for free, so don't worry about it," said Benjamin.

"Thanks Benji, but no one should work for free. You guys did a great job, and I'm not about to pay you in lemonade. Here, twenty dollars for you and twenty for Noogie. Thanks for everything guys," said Danny.

"So after you paid us you made a net profit of $206, right?"

"That's right Noogie, now you've got it!!"

"That's not bad bro! What are you going to do with all that money?" asked Benjamin.

"It's all going into the bank."

"IN THE BANK?!" Benjamin and Noogie yelled at the same time. "You mean you're not going to buy the new Zombie Killer video game or the ultra light titanium skateboard everybody's got?"

"Nope! It's all going in the bank. Dan, the Man, has got a plan! *Cha-Ching!* I'm not gonna become a millionaire by spending all my money on sneakers, skateboards and video games, but let's not get ahead of ourselves. We've got one more container of lemonade to go."

Net profits are the amount of money left after all expenses have been paid.

I KNOW WE'VE BEEN TALKING ABOUT MILLIONS IN DOLLARS, LET'S TALK ABOUT ONE MILLION IN TIME:
ONE MILLION SECONDS EQUALS 12 DAYS.
ONE MILLION MINUTES EQUALS 1 YEAR, 329 DAYS, 10 HOURS AND 40 MINUTES.
ONE MILLION HOURS AGO WAS IN 1885.

Chapter 9

The Mayor of Hurl

The boys were setting up the last container of lemonade when a big black limousine arrived. All the people from the festival rushed to see who was in it. The chauffeur opened the passenger door and four bodyguards in suits and sunglasses got out, followed by the Mayor of New York City. Suddenly, photographers and TV news people were all over the place.

'The Mayor never comes out to the hood,' Danny thought. *'He must be lost or up for re-election. Whoa! He's coming this way.'*

"Alright guys, this is our big chance to make a name for ourselves. Break out the last container of lemonade. We're gonna get the Mayor to buy a cup!" said Danny.

"Hey Mr. Mayor, how about a cup of the world's greatest lemonade!?" yelled Benjamin.

"Isn't this nice? Three young men working hard to make an honest dollar, I used to do the same when I was your age. What are your names, gentlemen?" asked the Mayor in a deep voice.

"This is Benjamin, that's Noogie, and I'm Danny, Danny Dollar. I'm the owner of the stand. It's nice to meet you, Mr. Mayor."

"It's very nice to meet you, Mr. Dollar. So how much is a cup of lemonade?"

"Just one dollar."

"I'll tell you what, young man. Here is a hundred dollar bill. Give one cup to my bodyguards, the media, one for me, and you keep the change," said the Mayor boastfully.

"YES SIR! COMING RIGHT UP!" Danny said excitedly.

The boys were so excited that they didn't notice the lemonade smelled a little funny, nor did they notice Pablo, Washington and Fingers laughing behind them. The Mayor and crew held their cups in the air to give Danny a toast.

"I am proud of your entrepreneurial spirit. Keep up the good work," said the Mayor. He took a big gulp then suddenly spit it out, spraying the entire crowd.

Then everybody started spitting out their lemonade. The bodyguards and TV crews were coughing and gagging. Danny, Noogie and Benjamin could only look on and wonder what in the world was going on?!

"Is this some kind of joke? This lemonade tastes like vinegar!"

"No way Mr. Mayor, this is the finest," exclaimed Danny, as he took a sip...and spit it out.

"It does taste like vinegar. What in the world? I don't know how this happened. I'm so sorry," Danny said shamefully.

"You should be sorry! This is unacceptable. It is not a good thing to play practical jokes on the Mayor. Give me back my money!" he shouted, snatching back his hundred dollar bill. He then jumped into his limo and sped away.

"How did vinegar get in the lemonade?" wondered Benjamin.

"I don't know. This is a disaster! Who would do this?" said Noogie.

The three boys suddenly looked at one another.

"PABLO!" they all shouted together.

DANNY'S DID YOU KNOW?

DID YOU KNOW THAT DOLLAR BILLS ARE NOT MADE OF PAPER? THEY ARE MADE OF 25 PERCENT LINEN AND 75 PERCENT COTTON. SINCE COTTON COMES FROM A PLANT, MAYBE MONEY REALLY DOES GROW ON TREES.

Chapter 10
Front Page Blues

Danny yawned as he got out of bed and headed downstairs for breakfast.

"Another day, another dollar," he grumbled.

"Good morning, honey. Did you sleep well?" asked Mom Dollar.

"No, I tossed and turned all night. I couldn't stop thinking about what happened with the Mayor yesterday. That was the worst day of my life," said Danny.

"Well son, this isn't going to make you feel any better, take a look at the front page of the newspaper," said Dad Dollar.

"AAAAAHHHHHH!" Danny yelled.

"*MAYOR RAINS ON PARADE!*"

shouted Danny, as he stared in horror at the picture of the mayor spitting out his lemonade and soaking the crowd.

"I can't believe this! That's it for me, I'm ruined. I'm never gonna be successful now. I'll forever be known as the kid who made the Mayor of New York City hurl," said Danny.

"What's the big deal, you make me wanna hurl every day," said Danielle.

Danny stormed out of the kitchen, ran into his bedroom and slammed the door hard enough to shake the house. Mom Dollar followed him to his room and knocked on the door.

"Hey sweetheart, can I talk to you?"

"Sure. Come in. I'm sorry I slammed

the door. I'm just a little upset with the whole lemonade incident. I really want to kick butt in everything I do, but all I did was look like a clown. I can never show my face outside again. Do you think I can be home-schooled and live with you and Dad 'til I'm 50?"

"No way, I don't want a 50-year-old

Lemonhead living in my house."

"MOM!" screamed Danny.

"Just kidding, honey! You have such a bright future. I know that all the dreams you have of becoming a millionaire and owning a basketball team are going to come true, but things are not always going to be easy. The road to success is usually a bumpy one. I guarantee that all self-made millionaires experienced adversity making it to the top. In fact, I bet if you ask them they will tell you that the hard times made them stronger and made them appreciate their success even more. When you make it big, I'm sure you will look back on the lemonade incident and laugh. Actually, you should be happy this even happened."

"Happy, why would I be happy, Mom?"

"You're famous now. Your picture is on the front page of the newspaper. Use it to your advantage," said Mom Dollar.

Suddenly, Danny's eyes began to twinkle.

"You're right, Mom. That gives me an idea, but I'm going to need your help," Danny said, brightening.

"Of course, honey. What do you need?"

"I need a ride to City Hall."

DANNY'S DID YOU KNOW?

DID YOU KNOW THAT THE UNITED STATES HAS MORE MILLIONAIRES THAN ANY OTHER COUNTRY IN THE WORLD AND NEW YORK CITY HAS MORE MILLIONAIRES THAN ANY CITY IN THE UNITED STATES? THAT MAKES NYC *CHA-CHING* CAPITAL OF THE WORLD!

Chapter 11
Making a Stand

Danny, Benjamin and Noogie whispered to each other in the car as they were being driven to City Hall.

"Danny, are you sure you know what you're doing?" asked Mom Dollar.

"I've never been surer. Hey, there's City Hall. Let us out right in front, okay?"

"All right boys, I'm just going to go park the car and I'll be right back."

"Don't worry, we'll have this all set up by the time you come back."

The boys quickly set up their lemonade stand right in front of City Hall.

"Get your ice-cold lemonade here! Ice-cold lemonade!" yelled Noogie and Benjamin, as a passerby stopped.

"Hey, I saw you guys on the front page of the paper. Aren't you the guys who made the Mayor throw up?"

"That wasn't our fault mister; we're here to show the city that we have the world's greatest lemonade. How about trying a cup? It only costs a buck."

"No thanks, kid. I don't have any health insurance."

"Very funny. Here, try a cup, no charge."

"I'm warning you kid, if I get sick, I'm telling my lawyer to sue you for every lemon you've got." He took a sip and then gulped down the rest. "Hey, that is good stuff, let me have another cup. Here's five bucks; you boys can keep the change."

"Thank you, mister."

"Hey boys, how's it going?" asked Mom Dollar.

"We just made our first sale of the day, Mrs. Dollar," said Benjamin.

"It's going to be a good day," stated Noogie.

"Get your ice-cold lemonade here!" shouted the boys.

"Excuse me, Mr. Mayor…"

"Yes, Mrs. Grant."

"There is something going on outside that I think you should see."

"What is it? I'm a little busy."

"Remember those boys who sold you lemonade the other day?"

"Yes, of course I do. How could I forget looking like a sprinkler on the front page of the newspaper. What about those boys?"

"They're in front of the building selling lemonade."

"THEY ARE WHAT?! This is an outrage. I will not be made a fool of!"

"You mean you will not be made a fool of twice."

"Mrs. Grant, call security and have them removed at once!"

"I would, but security is in line buying lemonade."

"This is ridiculous. I will handle this myself," stated the Mayor.

"We are really cleaning up!" said Benjamin. "I think we sold a cup of lemonade to every person in the city."

"Not yet, there's still one customer I'm looking for," said Danny.

"You're about to get your wish, honey, because the Mayor is walking this way, and he doesn't look happy," said Mom Dollar.

"Mr. Dollar!" shouted the Mayor. "You have got a lot of nerve coming here and selling that horrible excuse of a beverage. If you intend to further embarrass me, I must insist you take your friends and lemonade stand and go back to the Bronx!"

"Just one minute, Mr. Mayor!" said Mom Dollar.

"And who are you, Miss?" asked the Mayor.

"I'm Danny's mother, and if you would give the boys a chance, they'd like to explain something to you."

"Well, Mr. Dollar, what have you got to say for yourself?"

"Mr. Mayor, I apologize for what happened back at the festival. It really was an accident. You see, some guys put vinegar in my lemonade while my back was turned. I would never sell anyone contaminated lemonade on purpose. I take pride in all my jobs."

"All your jobs, how many jobs do you have?"

"You don't want to know," Mom Dollar said.

"Anyway, Mr. Mayor, I came here to show the city that Danny Dollar is a person of integrity and to say…sorry. I hope you can find it in your heart to forgive me."

"Well Mr. Dollar, can I call you Danny?

"Sure!" Danny said excitedly.

"It took a lot of spunk for you to come here to state your case. You are a special young man. Mrs. Dollar, you should be very proud of your son."

"I am, Mr. Mayor," Mom Dollar said with a grin.

"With that said, I'd be proud to have you and your friends as my guests at tonight's New York Ballers basketball game, if it's alright with your parents."

"WOOHOO!" Danny screamed. "Are you kidding, that would be awesome! Hey, wait a minute. The Ballers are playing the Mustangs tonight and the owner of the Mustangs, Rocky Austin, is my idol. Is he gonna be there?" asked Danny.

"As a matter of fact, Rocky is an old friend of mine; we went to college together. He will be in the skybox with us.

Now, is it still just one dollar for a cup of your lemonade? I'd love a nice cold..." The Mayor was interrupted by a loud thud.

"I'll get that for you sir, because my future millionaire son just fainted!" said Mom Dollar with a laugh.

DID YOU KNOW THE DENOMINATION AFTER A BILLION IS A TRILLION? BUT WHAT IS AFTER A TRILLION? CHECK THIS OUT:

MILLION 1,000,000
BILLION 1,000,000,000
TRILLION 1,000,000,000,000
QUADRILLION 1,000,000,000,000,000
QUINTILLION 1,000,000,000,000,000,000
SEXTILLION 1,000,000,000,000,000,000,000
SEPTILLION 1,000,000,000,000,000,000,000,000
OCTILLION 1,000,000,000,000,000,000,000,000,000
NONILLION 1,000,000,000,000,000,000,000,000,000,000

Chapter 12
The Skybox Rocks!

As Danny walked into the luxurious skybox, he was surprised to find Rocky Austin already there.

"Rocky, this is the young man I spoke to you about. I'd like you to meet Danny Dollar and his friends."

"Mr. Austin, you have no idea how much this means to me. I know every thing about you! I know where you were born: Pittsburgh, Pennsylvania. I know what college you went to: Indiana University. I even know your birthday: July 31st," Danny said joyfully.

"You know more about me than my Ma and Pa," Mr. Austin replied.

"These are my friends Noogie and Benjamin," Danny said.

"It's very nice to meet ya'll," Mr. Austin stated with a twang.

"Excuse me."

"Yes, um, is it Noogie?" Mr. Austin asked.

"Yep, that's me. Can I ask you a question? How did you get rich enough to buy a basketball team?"

"I wasn't always rich. As a young'un, I worked odd jobs to earn money and buy the things I wanted, like a nice pair of cowboy boots. After working in a fast food restaurant and having so much fun, I decided to open my own restaurant called Flippin' Burgers. It was a huge success, so I opened a Flippin' Burgers in every city across the country. I made so much money that I was able to invest into other restaurants and businesses. That's called......'

"DIVERISFYING!" Danny screamed out.

"Very impressive Danny, you must know a lot about finance."

"Yeah, I've got skills. I have a very **_diverse portfolio*_** of stocks, bonds, and **_mutual funds**_**," Danny said proudly.

"You do, huh? You seem a 'lil young to know so much about finances," Mr. Austin said in surprise.

"Finance is my thing. My goal is to be a millionaire and own my own basketball team just like you! And I'm gonna do it!"

"I reckon you will Danny. You know if you really want to see how a business is run, you can come by my office and I'll give you a tour. Here's my phone number.

You have your Ma or Pa give me a call and we'll set something up. In the meantime, the game is about to start and my Mustangs are about to stampede on them Ballers," Mr. Austin boasted.

"Oh, yeah?! The Ballers are gonna mop up the floor with your Mustangs."

"You wanna trash talk, kid? I can tangle with the best of them."

"Well then bring it, Mr. Austin," Danny yelled.

"You know what Danny, I've got a better idea, how's about a lil' wager?"

*Diverse portfolio – A wide variety of investments
**Mutual Funds – When an investment company takes money from a group of investors and invests it in a variety of stocks and bonds.

WHAT EXACTLY IS THE STOCK MARKET? THE WORD STOCK MEANS SUPPLIES, LIKE YOU HAVE A STOCK OF SNACKS IN YOUR PANTRY. THE WORD MARKET IS A PLACE WHERE THINGS ARE BOUGHT AND SOLD. THE STOCK MARKET IS NOT A PLACE. IT'S SIMPLY A TERM USED FOR THE BUSINESS OF BUYING AND SELLING STOCK.

Chapter 13
Way to go, CEO!

"Mom, Dad, yesterday was the best day of my life!"

"I'm sure it was, Son. Not many people get the chance to meet the person they most admire, much less hang out with them in their executive suite watching a basketball game," Dad Dollar said.

"Hanging out wasn't even the best part. The best part should be outside," Danny yelled with excitement.

"What should be outside?" Mom Dollar asked.

They all looked outside the window and saw a stretch limousine with a chauffeur standing behind it.

"Danny, what is this all about?" Dad Dollar asked.

"Mr. Austin said if his team lost he would let me be ***CEO**** of his company for a day, and the Mustangs got BLOWN OUT! PLEEEEEASE! CAN I GO?"

"Well, how can I say no? You can go, but under one condition," Dad Dollar said.

"Sure, Dad, anything!"

"Your sister has to go with you."

"What!?" Danny and Danielle shouted out together.

"I don't want to go anywhere with Dummy Dollar," Danielle said.

"Yeah, Dad, she'll just make my day a nightmare."

"If Danielle doesn't go, then you don't go. Take it or leave it," Mom Dollar said.

"I'll take it," Danny said glumly.

A professionally dressed woman was waiting for Danny and Danielle when they arrived at the office of Austin Enterprises.

"Good morning, Mr. and Ms. Dollar, we've been expecting you. I'm Alexandra Hamilton. I'll be your personal assistant for the day. Whatever you may need, I am here to assist with it."

"It's nice to meet you, but where's Mr. Austin?" Danny asked.

"Mr. Austin will not be with us today. There is a situation that needed his attention in our Texas office. He stated that you are in charge. I will show you to your office and brief you for a board of directors meeting that you are chairing in thirty minutes."

"A MEETING? BOARD OF DIRECTORS? ARE YOU JOKING? I can't run a meeting, I'm just a kid!" said Danny nervously.

"Mr. Austin seems to believe you are very capable. The meeting is about how to get more people to attend Mustang basketball games. Attendance has been very low this season, and Mr. Austin wants your input on how to increase it. Here is your office. I will be back in thirty minutes to bring you to the meeting, Mr. Dollar."

"AAAAHHHH! Danielle, how in the world can I lead a board meeting?" Danny shouted.

"I don't know, but since you're the boss, can you find out if you have an expense account? I would love to do some shopping!" Danielle asked.

"You're hopeless, why don't you go watch TV, I have to do some serious thinking."

"OOOOH TV, COOL!!" Danielle screamed.

Thirty minutes later, Ms. Hamilton came into the office. "Excuse me, Mr. Dollar, the Board is waiting for you."

"Okay, Alexandra, I'm ready." he said a bit nervously.

"Good luck," Ms. Hamilton whispered before Danny stepped into the boardroom.

"Ladies and Gentlemen, I'd like to present your CEO, Danny Dollar. That's your chair over there, sir." she said and pointed to a giant chair at the far end of the room before closing the door. Danny entered the large, luxurious boardroom where twelve well dressed men and women sat staring at him. He walked stiffly to the head of the table and stood beside a giant chair.

"You may have a seat, Mr. Dollar," said a stuffy old man.

"Ahhhh, this seat is big and cushy. Can you guys see me?" asked Danny.

Silence.....

"Members of the Board, the first thing I'd like to say is....***PPPRRRTTT***", Danny accidentally ripped a loud fart. "Oops! Sorry, I'm a little nervous. I did that once in front of my class after eating beans and franks for lunch in the school cafeteria, but that's another story."

Silence....

"Well, here's my idea. I'm 11 years old and a huge basketball fan. Basketball is my life. I'd like someone to guess how many professional basketball games I've been to? You sir, in the blue suit."

"Ten," said the man in the blue suit.

"Nope, fewer. How about you Ms., in the pink blouse?"

"Four?" asked the woman in the pink blouse.

"Nope, last try, you with the big thick

glasses."

"One?" guessed the man with the big glasses.

"Yep, only one and that was yesterday courtesy of the Mayor. Who can guess why?"

"Is it because the games are too expensive?" asked the man in the blue suit sarcastically.

"YOU GOT IT! My Dad would love to take me to a professional basketball game, but he is saving his money to put me and my older sister through college. Although just between us, my sister probably can't spell college.

Silence....

So here is the plan: KIDS FREE NIGHT!"

Everyone gasped in shock.

"That is ridiculous, Mr. Dollar. You do realize that we are not a charity. We are in the business of making money. We can not make money by giving away tickets. Whose idea was it to have this child here?" demanded the man in the blue suit.

"Look here, Mr. Stuffy, may I ask you a question?"

"Yes, you may…but my name is…." Danny interrupted before the man could continue.

"Have you ever gone anywhere that you usually paid to get into, but got in for free?"

"Why, yes I have."

"Where was it?"

"It was a movie theater. A colleague of mine had free passes to see *The English King*."

"The English King, what kind of movie is that?" asked Danny.

"It's a foreign film, Mr. Dollar."

"It figures," Danny said under his breath. "Mr. Stuffy, did you buy any food at the concession stand that day?"

"Yes, I did and I would greatly appreciate it if you would refer to me as Mr. Jefferson. I purchased a large popcorn, a large soda, a hot dog, nachos and some candy."

"Wow, Mr. Stuffy, I mean Mr. Jefferson, why did you buy so much food?"

"I figured since I saved money on the

movie I could spend a little extra on the food."

"Mr. Jefferson, you just made my point. If my Dad took me to see a basketball game and didn't have to pay for me to get in, I bet he would spend a little extra money on stuff like snacks and souvenirs. The money you would lose on ticket sales you would gain on extra's like food, jerseys and program books. Not only would you fill the seats, you would create a great image as an organization that cares about families and kids. Think about it, 'The Mustangs, the team that lets kids dream!' It's a win-win." Danny heard whispers around the boardroom.

"We will discuss your proposal with Mr.

Austin and let you know what he thinks," said Mr. Jefferson.

"I can already tell you what I think, Mr. Jefferson. It's a FANTASIC idea. Way to go, Danny!"

"Mr. Austin, is that you? Where are you?" asked Danny looking around the room.

"I'm on speaker phone. I was listening in on the whole meeting. Sorry I couldn't be there in person. I'm sure Alexandra apologized for me. I'd like to get on that idea right away. Danny, I knew there was something special 'bout you. When you get older, there'll be a job here for ya with Austin Enterprises. Maybe you can takeover Mr. Stuffy's position."

"Thank you, Mr. Austin, but I'll have my own business some day and when I do, you can come and work for me."

"Danny, are you trash talking again?"

"Mr. Austin, I am the boss, just for today anyway, and the boss is always right."

*CEO stands for Chief Executive Officer. The C.E.O. is the highest-ranking executive in a company or organization, in other words: The Boss! The Man! The Head Honcho! The Big Baller Shot Caller, got it?

DANNY'S DID YOU KNOW?

DID YOU KNOW THAT THE CHANCES OF YOU BECOMING A MILLIONAIRE HAVE NEVER BEEN BETTER? YOU DON'T NEED TO HIT THE LOTTERY OR HAVE A MULTI-PLATINUM SELLING RECORD. INSTEAD OF BUYING SNEAKERS, VIDEO GAMES OR JEWELRY, HAVE THE DISCIPLINE TO SAVE AND INVEST THE MONEY YOU EARN, THINK ABOUT IT? DO YOU KNOW ANY MILLIONAIRES? HOW COOL WOULD IT BE FOR YOU TO BE ONE?

Chapter 14
Bucks for Ducks

Yawn. "Another day, another dollar. Morning, Mom."

"Good morning, honey. Are you still wound-up from working for Mr. Austin yesterday?"

"Yep, working in that big office, being in charge of a meeting and a staff of executives was pretty cool. It gave me an idea of what it feels like to run a real business and made me really excited about the future, but I'm just as excited about today."

"Why sweetheart, what have you got going on today?"

"The guys and I are having a car wash and ten percent of our earnings will go towards feeding the homeless."

"That is so nice Danny, I'm proud of you," said Mom Dollar.

"Yep, it's gonna be great, and we have a secret weapon that is gonna generate lots of money."

"What's your secret weapon?"

"I'll show you Mom. Hey Danielle, are you ready?" Danny yelled out.

"Do I have to come out there?" screamed Danielle from her room.

"Yep, a deal is a deal," Danny shouted.

Danielle finally came out of her room dressed like a giant duck.

"Danielle, why in the world are you dressed liked that?" Mom Dollar asked.

"I had to borrow a few bucks from Danny yesterday. He said I wouldn't have to pay him back if I wore this outfit to attract customers while his team of misfits washes cars. I feel ridiculous!" yelled Danielle.

"You look ridiculous!" giggled Danny.

"Let this be a lesson to you, Danielle. When you borrow money, one way or another, you are going to pay."

The Closing Bell

Wow! The past few days have been crazy. One day the Mayor of New York City is gagging on my lemonade, a few days later, I'm thinking up million dollar ideas for my idol, and now mentor, Rocky Austin.

It just goes to show, you could be dealing with something that might seem like the worst thing in the world, but could turn out to be a blessing in disguise. If Pablo and his friends hadn't put vinegar in my lemonade, I might have never met Mr. Austin.

Mom was right. Things are not always gonna be easy in life. You just have to believe in yourself and never, ever give up.

So, my friends out there, what did we learn today? Regardless of how old you are, if you're creative enough, there are plenty of ways to make a couple of bucks, whether it's through your allowance, opening a lemonade stand, or walking a neighbor's dog.

Take a good amount of the money you've earned and open up a bank account. Set goals for how much you can save each year, and tell your friends and relatives that for your birthday and holidays to forget the toys and games because "Cash is King."

Investing is a great way to make money. There are plenty of things to invest in like stocks, bonds, and even real estate; don't let this stuff intimidate you. Talk to your parents about it, maybe you can invest together. Find a way to make that paper. ***Cha-ching!***

Remember, having sneakers that cost a lot of dollars does not make a lot of sense. Just ask Pablo.

Also, think twice about borrowing money when you can't afford to pay it back. You can put yourself into a big hole of debt that can be really hard to get out of. Danielle had to find that out the hard way and ended up looking like an ugly duckling.

Money is important. It's not the most important thing in the world, but it's important enough to start thinking about it now! You've got to plan—plan how to make money, plan how to save, plan how to spend, and plan to invest for your future. It will be here before you know it. I know I'll be ready, will you?

Peace out from Dan, the Man with the Plan. I'll holla!

WHAT'S YOUR PLAN ON HOW
TO BECOME A MILLIONAIRE?
TELL THE WORLD AT
DANNYDOLLAR.COM OR FIND
ME ON FACEBOOK AT DANNY
DOLLAR MILLIONAIRE
EXTRAORDINAIRE

ACKNOWLEDGEMENTS

This book would not have been possible
without the inspiration of my wife,
Martique Jackson and sister,
Nicole Davies.

Thank you to Jon Shears for working on
this project and helping make my dream
come to life.

Thank you to the people mentioned in this
book: Farrah Gray, Bill and Melinda Gates
and Mark Cuban, who was my inspiration
for Rocky Austin.

Oh! Hi, Mom!

ABOUT THE AUTHOR

Ty Allan Jackson was born and raised in the Bronx, New York, and as a child loved to read. Now, as the founder of BiG HeAd BoOkS, his mission is to introduce children of all cultures to the fun and empowerment of reading. He lives in Western Massachusetts with his beautiful wife, son, two daughters and is a big-time mama's boy.

ABOUT THE ILLUSTRATOR

Jonathan Shears grew up in a small town commonly known as "Wrinkle City". He later spent several years in Boston, Massachusetts pursuing his artistic career, where his story as the real-life Nacho Libre began. Jonathan is an active member within his home church, and is a lifelong professional wrestling fan. At one time, he was following his passion by performing in the ring, until injury sent him in a different direction. Now, you can find him training for bodybuilding competitions and designing for the web.